Staying Alive

WRITTEN BY
ANN HARTH

ILLUSTRATED BY
DION HAMILL

SERIES EDITORS
MITCH AND GLYN O'TOOLE

highlights!

Staying Alive
ISBN: 1 86509 040 9

Written by Ann Harth
Illustrated by Dion Hamill
Copyright © 2005 Blake Publishing and Ann Harth

Published by Blake Education Pty Ltd
ABN 50 074 266 023
108 Main Rd
Clayton South VIC 3168
Ph: (03) 9558 4433
Fax: (03) 9558 5433
email: mail@blake.com.au
Visit our website: www.blake.com.au

Series publisher: Katy Pike

Highlights! program developed by UC Publishing Pty Ltd
Designers: Luke Sharrock and Craig Longmuir
Series editors: Mitch and Gjyn O'Toole

Printed by Printing Creations

Contents

1. The Island

Nalini hears the bats come into the cave. She opens her eyes.

"Are you awake, Nalini?" Zed says.

"I'm awake." Nalini stretches her arms and stands up. She has a drink from a coconut. "How is your arm?" she asks.

"It's stiff," Zed says. "But it gets better every day. Watch me move my fingers."

Nalini watches Zed bend his thumb a little.

"Good," she says. "I think that means it's not broken."

Zed picks up a stick and draws a fourth line on the dirt floor. "This is our fourth day since the aeroplane crashed," he says. "They must be looking for us."

Nalini empties the coconut over her hand.

"I have to get more water today," she says.

A pile of cracked coconuts is on the floor. Nalini uses a piece of steel from the plane to peel the skin from the coconuts. Then she smashes them open with a stone.

Nalini looks outside. "Zed, your sign is almost gone."

Zed sighs. "I know," he says. "I'll make another one today."

"I wish we could make a fire. Smoke is easier to see. If we had a fire, they could see us and rescue us," Nalini says.

Later, Nalini sees the sea water is down the beach, away from the trees.

"The tide is going out, Zed," she says. "I have to go." She takes three empty coconuts and jumps onto the beach.

The sun is hot. Nalini walks to the stream. She enters the cool, dark trees and reaches the pool. She sits on a rock with her feet in the water.

She pulls the coconuts from the backpack and fills them with water. She lies on her stomach and splashes water on her face. The sunlight sparkles on the pool.

Suddenly, the light disappears. Nalini stares. A shadow moves across the water. She stands up and looks at the top of the waterfall.

Nothing moves.

Is there something there? Are there dangerous animals on the island? Nalini quickly puts the coconuts into the backpack and hurries away from the pool.

9

2. A Plane and Fruit

It is early the next morning.

"Listen," Zed whispers. They run outside.

"There!" Nalini points to a dark spot in the sky. It moves closer and the sound grows louder.

"It's a plane, Nalini!" Zed looks down at the beach. "But our sign is gone," he says. He waves his good arm and shouts at the plane.

Nalini calls and waves both arms. The plane flies in large circles over the water. Nalini calls and calls.

The plane circles again and again. Then it flies away. Nalini feels a tear fall on her cheek. She looks at Zed. His eyes look wet too.

"If we had a fire, they could find us," he says.

Nalini enters the cave and lies down. Tears fill her eyes. She closes her eyes and pretends she is at home in bed.

When Nalini wakes up, she has to collect more water. She takes the coconuts and backpack outside. Zed's eyes are red. He tries to make a fire.

Nalini walks slowly to the pool. "Will we ever leave this island and see our family again?" she thinks.

It is dark near the pool. Nalini fills her coconuts and turns to leave. She stops. There is some fruit near the edge of the pool. Nalini steps closer.

She remembers the shadow from yesterday. Nalini picks up a purple piece of fruit. "Is it poisonous?" she wonders.

Nalini squeezes juice from a small berry onto her tongue. It tastes sweet.

"If I don't get sick, I will eat one," Nalini says. She puts the fruit in her backpack and walks back to the cave.

"Zed, look!" Nalini says. She puts the fruit on the rocks.

"Where did you find those?" Zed asks.

"I found them at the pool. I had a drop of berry juice. I haven't tasted the purple things yet."

Zed picks up one and takes a tiny bite.

"If we're not sick tomorrow we can eat a bit more," Nalini says.

"That's good," Zed says. "I'm tired of eating coconuts."

They lie down and go to sleep.

3. We're Not Alone

Zed draws the ninth line on the floor. Twice, the plane came at high tide. The seaweed sign was gone both times. They need a fire.

Every day, Nalini and Zed collect water and open coconuts. They make seaweed signs and they try to start a fire.

Nalini says, "I want to find the fruit trees, today. You get water."

Zed goes to the pool and Nalini walks slowly behind him.

As she walks along the sand, something runs into the rainforest beside her. Nalini takes a step into the forest and falls over a log.

"Ouch!" She sits on the log and rubs her ankle.

There's some fruit on the log beside her. She picks up the berries and runs onto the beach.

"Look, Zed!" Nalini runs after him.

"You found the fruit trees," Zed says.

"No, I didn't. These were in a pile on a log," Nalini says.

Zed is quiet. When they reach the pool, Zed fills the coconuts. Nalini steps into the water. She hears Zed shout.

"What's wrong?" Nalini swims towards Zed.

"Look," says Zed. He holds out a basket. It is big enough to carry four coconuts. It is woven from green leaves.

"Nalini," Zed says, "we're not alone."

Nalini and Zed leave the basket and run back to the cave.

"Who do you think it is?" Nalini asks.

"I don't know." Zed shakes his head.

Nalini looks at the sea. "I think the person wants to help us."

"How do you know that?" Zed sounds angry. Nalini knows he gets angry when he is afraid.

"I don't," Nalini says, "but remember the fruit? Remember the coconuts that had holes in them? Maybe the basket is for us."

"Maybe. But I think we should be careful. We should stay together."

"Yes," Nalini nods. "We will."

The wind blows hard. A coconut rolls off the rocks and plops into the water.

Zed stands up. "Here comes another storm. Let's go inside."

They walk into the cave.

21

4. The Storm

Nalini and Zed sit in the cave and watch the storm. The waves crash against the rocks. The wind blows and the sky turns black.

Nalini and Zed lean against the cave wall. Their shoulders touch.

"It's OK," Nalini says. "We're safe in here."

The lightning flashes. The thunder doesn't stop.

There is a noise from the back of the cave. Something moves. It sounds like feet on the floor.

Nalini squeezes Zed's shoulder.

The sound stops.

In the centre of the cave, there is a clink and a flicker. Nalini smells smoke. She sits up and stares at a small flame. Someone puts sticks on the fire and it grows stronger.

A small person with no hair and a long, white beard sits down on the other side of the fire.

"I am Nu," he says.

Nalini and Zed move closer together.

The man places his hand on his chest. "Nu," he says again.

"Nu?" Nalini says. She puts her hand on her own chest. "Nalini," she says. She points to her brother. "Zed."

Nu nods and puts another stick on the fire. He pulls his beard away from the flame. "Did you come on a boat?"

"No," Nalini says. "We were in an aeroplane. It crashed."

"It is good you are alive," Nu says.

"Yes."

Zed and Nalini move closer to the fire.

25

"Why are you on the island?" Zed asks.

Nu stares into the flames. "I choose to be here."

"How long have you been here?" Nalini asks.

"Twenty years."

Lightning flashes.

"Twenty years? But why?" Nalini looks at Nu. There are deep lines around his eyes and mouth. "Do you miss your family?"

"My family." Nu closes his eyes.

Nalini and Zed are quiet. Lightning flashes again. The thunder is loud.

"My wife," Nu says. "My boys. They died in an accident." Nu talks slowly. It seems like he is remembering how to talk.

"I'm sorry," Zed says.

5. The Stranger

Nalini looks into the fire.

Nu speaks again. "After my family died, I bought a boat and left my home. My boat hit a rock and sank. I swam here."

"Just like us," Nalini says. "Did you try to get home?"

"Never."

"We want to go home," Zed says.

"Did you leave the coconuts and fruit for us?" Zed asks.

"I did," Nu says. "I made the basket, too."

Nalini smiles at the small man. "Thank you," she says.

"You still need to learn," says Nu. "The wet season is close."

"Oh, we won't be here long. We will be rescued very soon."

29

Nu is quiet.

Zed leans forward. "We will be rescued if we can make a fire. Will you show us how?" he asks.

"It is difficult to make a fire," Nu says.

"Will you show us which fruit we can eat and how to make baskets?"

"I will show you these things. But now I will sleep." Nu lies down on his side with his back near the fire. He curls into a ball.

Zed and Nalini lie down too but Nalini can't sleep. The storm is loud and there is a strange, little man nearby. She watches the light from the flames flicker on Nu's shiny head.

At last her eyes close.

In the morning, the storm is over.

Nu is gone.

"Zed!" Nalini rubs her eyes. "Nu's gone!"

Zed sits up and picks up a stick. He stirs the coals of the fire. "I hope he comes back soon," Zed says. "I want to learn to start a fire."

Nalini and Zed walk outside. Branches and leaves cover their rock. Nalini throws a stick into the sea.

"No, Nalini," Zed says. "We will need them for our fire."

They put the wood in a pile at the edge of the rock. Nu is nowhere to be seen.

"Where could Nu be?" Nalini looks down at the beach. "I don't see any footprints in the sand."

6. Another Cave

Nu walks out of the cave onto their rock.

"How did you get inside?" Zed asks.

"I will show you," Nu says. He walks to the crack in the back of the cave. He squeezes through. "Come through," Nu calls.

They squeeze through the narrow crack to the rainforest behind their cave. "We have a secret back door," Nalini says.

"Come," says Nu.

Nalini and Zed run behind him up a hill, until Nu stops in front of a rock wall. Nu steps behind a large stone and disappears.

"Nu?" Zed and Nalini walk around the stone to an opening in the wall.

"I'm in here," Nu's voice comes from the opening.

Zed and Nalini walk into a small stone room.

Nalini looks around. A circle of black coals is on the floor and many coconuts are against one wall. "It's smaller and stuffier than the other cave," she says.

"This is my wet season cave," Nu says.

"The other one is nicer," Nalini says. "Why did you leave it?"

Nu says, "When the wet season comes, it rains for weeks. The cave fills with water. The bats can stay there but I can't."

Nalini bites her lip. "When does the wet season start?"

Nu looks at both children. "It starts with very hot days and storms at night."

"But that's happening now," Nalini says.

"Yes," says Nu.

They go outside.

Zed throws a stone against the rock wall. "Should we move away from the beach?" he asks.

Nu nods. "If you aren't rescued soon, the planes won't be able to get here. You will have to stay here until the wet season finishes."

"How long is that?" Nalini says.

"Sometimes it lasts for months. I store food now, for when the weather is bad. Sometimes I can't leave the cave for weeks."

Zed and Nalini stand up. Nalini says, "We must make our sign. We have to be rescued soon."

Zed asks. "Will you show us how to make a fire so the rescue planes can find us?"

"It is difficult," says Nu.

7. A Fire

Nalini walks back down the hill. She wants to be rescued. She doesn't want to live in that small cave for months.

Nalini hears a sound. It's a small, buzzing sound. She runs to their cave. Zed is right behind her. Nu is slower.

She looks into the sky.

"Hurry, Zed!" she calls. "A plane!"

Nalini and Zed run to their cave. Nalini grabs some seaweed. She climbs onto the rock ledge and puts the seaweed in a pile. Zed puts small sticks on top.

The sound of the plane is louder.

"Quick!" Zed calls. "Bring the metal you use to open coconuts. It's made of steel."

Nalini runs inside as Nu comes in the back door of the cave. "Hurry, Nu! There's a plane. Help us make a fire."

Nu takes the metal from Nalini and steps onto the rocks.

"Sit down, Zed."

Zed sits on the ledge.

"Now put the flint stone on top of the seaweed."

Zed holds up three dark grey stones. "I found these outside the cave."

"Hurry, Nu." Nalini says. "The plane is closer. It is lower. Hurry."

Nu chooses a stone and gives it to Zed. "This should do it," he says. "Hit the stone with the metal. Hit it hard and fast. You should get some sparks."

"Go, Zed!" Nalini jumps up and down. She waves her arms at the plane and looks at the empty beach. "I wish we had a sign."

The stone hits the metal and clinks.

"I saw a spark!" Nalini yells. The spark lands on the seaweed. It makes a thin line of smoke. Then it disappears.

"Again, Zed. Keep going!" Nalini looks up at the plane. It circles again.

Zed hits the metal again and again. Nalini doesn't want the plane to leave. Nalini shouts and waves her arms. She smells smoke and turns around.

A small flame burns in the middle of the seaweed. Nu blows on the flame and it grows.

"You made a fire, Zed!" Nalini shouts. She calls to the plane. "Look! We're here!" Nalini watches the plane make one last circle.

"No! Come back!" Nalini yells. "Zed, they didn't see us. We need more smoke. We need a bigger fire."

"We are too late," Zed says. He looks into his fire.

Nalini stares into the sky. "We were almost rescued. You made a fire," Nalini says.

Zed looks up at her. "That's true. Now we can make a fire. We'll keep it burning all the time."

Nalini puts a handful of seaweed onto the flames. A cloud of smoke rises into the sky.

"The next time a plane comes, we'll be ready," Nalini says.